Other Books by Roald Dahl

ROALD DAHL

The Enormous Crocodile

Illustrated by Quentin Blake

JONATHAN CAPE
London

First published 1978

Text © 1978 by Roald Dahl Nominee Ltd
Illustration © 1978 by Quentin Blake

This edition published in 1999 by
Jonathan Cape Ltd, 20 Vauxhall Bridge Road,
London SW1V 2SA

A CIP catalogue record for this book
is available from the British Library

ISBN 0-2240-4684-5

Printed in Singapore

Danny, The Champion of the World was
the first book by Roald Dahl to be published
by Jonathan Cape. That was in 1975. Not long
thereafter I asked Roald whether he would
consider writing a short text for a colour picture
book. He said he had already tried and found it
'damned difficult' - even more difficult than writing
a children's novel. I continued to pester him,
insisting that with his remarkable gift he could
bring something fabulous to the picture book.
And then one day, one glorious day, three years
later, he handed me some pages of a manuscript
entitled *The Enormous Crocodile* or 'The Enormous
Croc' as he put it. It is a wonderful story.

Now, what we needed was an illustrator.
Roald came to my office and I laid out the work
of various artists we published plus a number of
others. I was delighted when after much discussion
he decided in favour of Quentin Blake. It was the
choice I would have made. And so with this book
we have a double first. *The Enormous Crocodile* is
Roald Dahl's first picture book for children. It is
also the first book by Roald Dahl to be illustrated
by Quentin Blake. This 'marriage' to Quentin
lasted throughout Roald's lifetime. It was an
enormously successful and also a very happy
experience for both the writer and artist. And for
my part it has turned out to be a piece of
matchmaking of which I am especially proud.

TOM MASCHLER

In the biggest brownest muddiest river in Africa, two crocodiles lay with their heads just above the water. One of the crocodiles was enormous. The other was not so big.

"Do you know what I would like for my lunch today?" the Enormous Crocodile asked.

"No," the Notsobig One said. "What?"

The Enormous Crocodile grinned, showing hundreds of sharp white teeth. "For my lunch today," he said, "I would like a nice juicy little child."

"I never eat children," the Notsobig One said. "Only fish."

"Ho, ho, ho!" cried the Enormous Crocodile. "I'll bet if you saw a fat juicy little child paddling in the water over there at this very moment, you'd gulp him up in one gollop!"

"No, I wouldn't," the Notsobig One said. "Children are too tough and chewy. They are tough and chewy and nasty and bitter."

"Tough and chewy!" cried the Enormous Crocodile. "Nasty and bitter! What awful tommy-rot you talk! They are juicy and yummy!"

"They taste so bitter," the Notsobig One said, "you have to cover them with sugar before you can eat them."

"Children are bigger than fish," said the Enormous Crocodile. "You get bigger helpings."

"You are greedy," the Notsobig One said. "You're the greediest croc in the whole river."

"I'm the bravest croc in the whole river," said the Enormous Crocodile. "I'm the only one who dares to leave the water and go through the jungle to the town to look for little children to eat."

"You've only done that once," snorted the Notsobig One. "And what happened then? They all saw you coming and ran away."

"Ah, but today when I go, they won't see me at all," said the Enormous Crocodile.

"Of course they'll see you," the Notsobig One said. "You're so enormous and ugly, they'll see you from miles away."

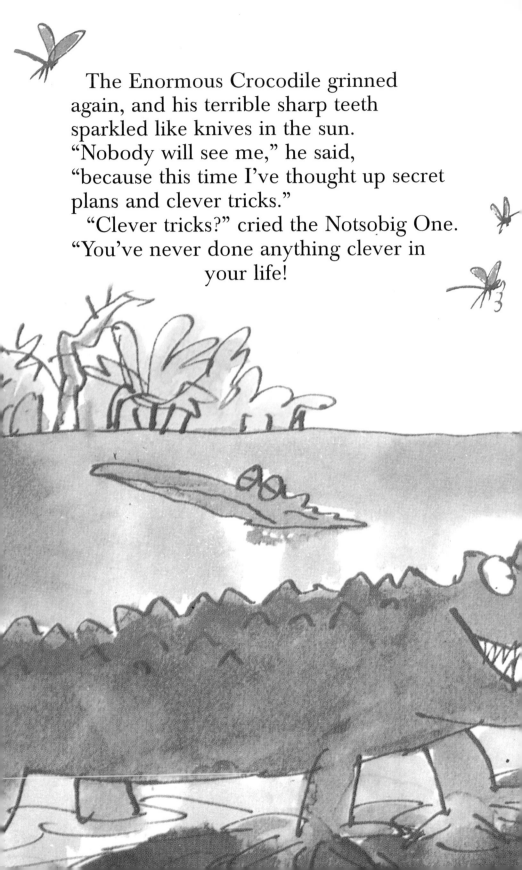

The Enormous Crocodile grinned
again, and his terrible sharp teeth
sparkled like knives in the sun.
"Nobody will see me," he said,
"because this time I've thought up secret
plans and clever tricks."

"Clever tricks?" cried the Notsobig One.
"You've never done anything clever in
your life!

You're the stupidest croc on the whole river!"

"I'm the cleverest croc on the whole river," the Enormous Crocodile answered. "For my lunch today I shall feast upon a fat juicy little child while you lie here in the river feeling hungry. Goodbye."

The Enormous Crocodile swam to the side of the river, and crawled out of the water.

A gigantic creature was standing
in the slimy oozy mud on the river-bank.
It was Humpy-Rumpy, the
Hippopotamus.
"Hello, hello," said Humpy-Rumpy.
"Where on earth are you off to at this
time of day?"
"I have secret plans and clever tricks,"
said the Crocodile.
"Oh dear," said Humpy-Rumpy.
"I'll bet you're going to do
something horrid."

The Enormous Crocodile grinned at
Humpy-Rumpy and said:

*"I'm going to fill my
hungry empty tummy
With something yummy
yummy yummy yummy!"*

"What's so yummy?" asked Humpy-Rumpy.

"Try to guess," said the Crocodile. "It's something that walks on two legs."

"You don't mean…" said Humpy-Rumpy. "You don't really mean you're going to eat a little child?"

"Of course I am," said the Crocodile.

"Oh, you horrid greedy grumptious brute!" cried Humpy-Rumpy. "I hope you get caught and cooked and turned into crocodile soup!"

The Enormous Crocodile laughed out loud at Humpy-Rumpy. Then he waddled off into the jungle.

Inside the jungle, he met Trunky, the Elephant. Trunky was nibbling leaves from the top of a tall tree, and he didn't notice the Crocodile at first. So the Crocodile bit him on the leg.

"Ow!" said Trunky in his big deep voice. "Who did that? Oh, it's you, is it, you beastly Crocodile. Why don't you go back to the big brown muddy river where you belong?"

"I have secret plans and clever tricks," said the Crocodile.

"You mean you've nasty plans and nasty tricks," said Trunky. "You've never done a nice thing in your life."

The Enormous Crocodile grinned up at Trunky and said:

*"I'm off to find a yummy
child for lunch.
Keep listening and you'll hear
the bones go crunch!"*

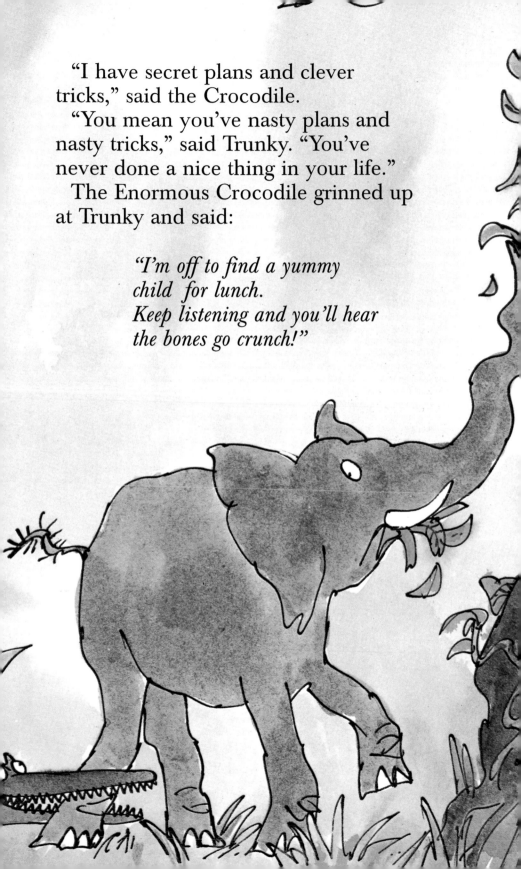

"Oh, you wicked beastly beast!" cried
Trunky. "Oh, you foul and filthy fiend!
I hope you get squashed and squished
and squizzled and boiled up into
crocodile stew!"

The Enormous Crocodile laughed out
loud and disappeared into the thick
jungle.

A bit further on, he met Muggle-Wump,
the Monkey. Muggle-Wump was sitting
in a tree, eating nuts.

"Hello, Crocky," said Muggle-Wump. "What are you up to now?"

"I have secret plans and clever tricks," said the Crocodile.

"Would you like some nuts?" asked Muggle-Wump.

"I have better things to eat than nuts," sniffed the Crocodile.

"I didn't think there was anything better than nuts," said Muggle-Wump.

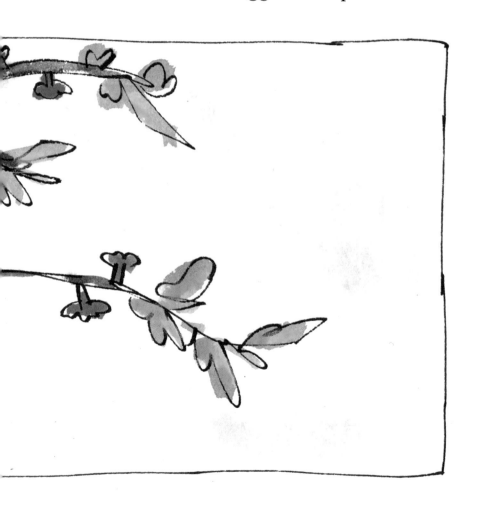

"Ah-ha," said the Enormous Crocodile,

> *"The sort of things that*
> *I'm going to eat*
> *Have fingers, toe-nails, arms*
> *and legs and feet!"*

Muggle-Wump went pale and began to shake all over. "You aren't really going to gobble up a little child, are you?" he said.

"Of course I am," said the Crocodile.

"Clothes and all. They taste better with the clothes on."

"Oh, you horrid hoggish croc!" cried Muggle-Wump.

"You slimy creature! I hope the buttons and buckles all stick in your throat and choke you to death!"

The Crocodile grinned up at Muggle-Wump and said, "I eat monkeys, too." And quick as a flash, with one bite of his huge jaws, he bit through the tree that Muggle-Wump was sitting in, and down it came.

But just in time,
Muggle-Wump jumped
into the next tree and swung away
through the branches.

A bit further on, the
Enormous Crocodile met
the Roly-Poly Bird. The
Roly-Poly Bird was building
a nest in an orange tree.

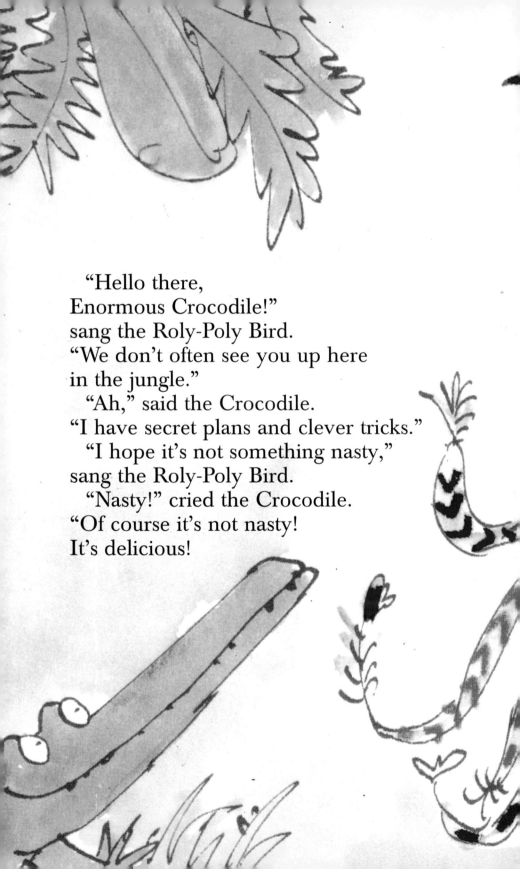

"Hello there,
Enormous Crocodile!"
sang the Roly-Poly Bird.
"We don't often see you up here
in the jungle."

"Ah," said the Crocodile.
"I have secret plans and clever tricks."

"I hope it's not something nasty,"
sang the Roly-Poly Bird.

"Nasty!" cried the Crocodile.
"Of course it's not nasty!
It's delicious!

"It's luscious, it's super,
It's mushious, it's duper,
It's better than rotten old fish.
You mash it and munch it,
You chew it and crunch it!
It's lovely to hear it go squish!"

"It must be berries," sang the Roly-Poly
Bird. "Berries are my favourite food in
the world. Is it raspberries, perhaps?
Or could it be strawberries?"

The Enormous Crocodile laughed so
much his teeth rattled together like
pennies in a moneybox. "Crocodiles
don't eat berries," he said. "We eat little
boys and girls. And sometimes we eat
Roly-Poly Birds, as well." Very quickly,
the Crocodile reached up and snapped
his jaws at the Roly-Poly Bird.

He just missed the Bird, but he
managed to catch hold of the long
beautiful feathers in its tail.
The Roly-Poly Bird gave a shriek of
terror and shot straight up into the air,
leaving its tail feathers behind in the
Enormous Crocodile's mouth.

26

At last, the Enormous Crocodile came
out of the other side of the jungle into
the sunshine. He could see the town not
far away.

"Ho-ho!" he said, talking aloud to
himself. "Ha-ha! that walk through the

jungle has made me hungrier than ever.
One child isn't going to be nearly enough
for me today. I won't be full up until I've
eaten at least three juicy little children."

He started to creep forward towards the
town.

The Enormous Crocodile crept over to
a place where there were a lot of coconut
trees.

He knew that children from the town
often came here looking for coconuts.
The trees were too tall for them to climb,
but there were always some coconuts on
the ground that had fallen down.

The Enormous Crocodile quickly
collected all the coconuts that were lying
on the ground. He also gathered together
several fallen branches.

"Now for Clever Trick Number One!"
he whispered to himself. "It won't be long
before I am eating the first part of my
lunch!"

He took all the coconut branches and
held them between his teeth.

He grasped the coconuts in his front
paws. Then he stood straight up in the
air, balancing himself on his tail.

He arranged the branches and the coconuts so cleverly that he now looked exactly like a small coconut tree standing among the big coconut trees.

Soon, two children came along. They were brother and sister. The boy was called Toto. His sister was called Mary. They walked around looking for fallen coconuts, but they couldn't find any because the Enormous Crocodile had gathered them all up.

"Oh look!" cried Toto. "That tree over there is much smaller than the others! And it's full of coconuts! I think I could climb that one quite easily if you help me up the first bit."

Toto and
Mary ran towards
what they thought was
the small coconut tree.
The Enormous
Crocodile peered
through the branches,
watching them as they
came closer and closer.
He licked his lips. He
began to dribble
with excitement.

Suddenly there was a tremendous whooshing noise. It was Humpy-Rumpy, the Hippopotamus. He came crashing and snorting out of the jungle. His head was down low and he was galloping at a terrific speed.

"Look out, Toto!" shouted Humpy-Rumpy. "Look out, Mary! That's not a coconut tree! It's the Enormous Crocodile and he wants to eat you up!"

Humpy-Rumpy charged straight at the Enormous Crocodile.

He caught him with his giant head and sent him tumbling and skidding over the ground.

"Ow-eeee!" cried the Crocodile. "Help! Stop! Where am I?"

Toto and Mary ran back to the town as fast as they could.

But crocodiles are tough. It is difficult for even a hippopotamus to hurt them.

The Enormous Crocodile picked himself up and crept towards the place where the children's playground was.

"Now for Clever Trick Number Two!" he said to himself. "This one is certain to work!"

There were no children in the playground at that moment. They were all in school.

The Enormous Crocodile found a large piece of wood and placed it in the middle of the playground. Then he lay across the piece of wood and tucked in his feet so that he looked almost exactly like a see-saw.

When school was over, the children all came running on to the playground.

"Oh look!" they cried. "We've got a new see-saw!"

They all crowded round, shouting with excitement.

"Bags I have the first go!"

"I'll get on the other end!"

"I want to go first!"

"So do I! So do I!"

Then, a girl who was older than the others said, "It's rather a funny knobbly sort of a see-saw, isn't it? Do you think it'll be safe to sit on?"

"Of course it will!" the others said. "It looks strong as anything!"

The Enormous Crocodile opened one eye just a tiny bit and watched the children who were crowding around him.

Soon, he thought, one of them is going to sit on my head, then I will give a jerk and a snap, and after that it will be *yum yum yum*.

At that moment, there was a flash of brown and something jumped into the playground and hopped up on to the top of the swings.

It was Muggle-Wump, the Monkey.

"Run!" Muggle-Wump shouted to the children. "All of you, run, run, run!

That's not a see-saw! It's the Enormous Crocodile and he wants to eat you up!"

The children screamed and ran for their lives.

Muggle-Wump disappeared back into the jungle, and the Enormous Crocodile was left all alone in the playground.

He cursed the Monkey and waddled back into the bushes to hide.

"I'm getting hungrier and hungrier!" he said. "I shall have to eat at least four children now before I am full up!"

The Enormous Crocodile crept around the edge of the town, taking great care not to be seen.

He came to a place where they were
getting ready to have a fair. There were
slides and swings and dodgem-cars and
people selling popcorn and candy-floss.
There was also a big roundabout.

The roundabout had marvellous
wooden creatures for the children to ride
on. There were white horses and lions
and tigers and mermaids with fishes' tails
and fearsome dragons with red tongues
sticking out of their mouths.

"Now for Clever Trick Number Three,"

said the Enormous Crocodile, licking his lips.

When no one was looking, he crept up on to the roundabout and put himself between a wooden lion and a fearsome dragon. He sat up a bit on his back legs and he kept very still. He looked exactly like a wooden crocodile on the roundabout.

Soon, all sorts of children came flocking into the fair. Several of them ran towards the roundabout. They were very excited.

"I'm going to ride on a dragon!" cried one.

"I'm going on a lovely white horse!" cried another.

"I'm going on a lion!" cried a third one.

And one little girl, whose name was Jill, said, "I'm going to ride on that funny old wooden crocodile!"

The Enormous Crocodile kept very still, but he could see the little girl coming towards him. "Yummy-yum-yum," he thought. "I'll gulp her up easily in one gollop."

Suddenly there was a swish and a swoosh and something came swishing and swooshing out of the sky.

It was the Roly-Poly Bird.

He flew round and round the roundabout, singing, "Look out, Jill! Look out! Look out! Don't ride on that crocodile!"

Jill stopped and looked up.

"That's not a wooden crocodile!" sang the Roly-Poly Bird. "It's a real one! It's the Enormous Crocodile from the river and he wants to eat you up!"

Jill turned and ran. So did all the other children. Even the man who was working the roundabout jumped off it and ran away as fast as he could.

The Enormous Crocodile cursed the Roly-Poly Bird and waddled back into the bushes to hide.

"I'm so hungry now," he said to himself, "I could eat six children before I am full up!"

Just outside the town, there was a pretty little field with trees and bushes all round it. This was called The Picnic Place. There were several wooden tables and long benches, and people were allowed to go there and have a picnic at any time.

The Enormous Crocodile crept over to The Picnic Place. There was no one in sight.

"Now for Clever Trick Number Four!" he whispered to himself.

He picked a lovely bunch of flowers and arranged it on one of the tables.

From the same table, he took away one of the benches and hid it in the bushes.

Then he put himself in the place where the bench had been.

By tucking his head under his chest, and by twisting his tail out of sight, he made himself look very much like a long wooden bench with four legs.

Soon two boys and two girls came along carrying baskets of food. They were all from one family, and their mother had said they could go out and have a picnic together.

"Which table shall we sit at?" said one.

"Let's take the table with the lovely flowers on it," said another.

The Enormous Crocodile kept as quiet
as a mouse. "I shall eat them all," he said
to himself. "They will come and sit on
my back and I will swizzle my head
around quickly, and after that it'll be
squish crunch gollop."

46

47

Suddenly a big deep voice from the jungle shouted, "Stand back, children! Stand back! Stand back!"

The children stopped and stared at the place where the voice was coming from.

Then, with a crashing of branches, Trunky the Elephant came rushing out of the jungle.

"That's not a bench you were going to sit on!" he bellowed. "It's the Enormous Crocodile, and he wants to eat you all up!"

Trunky trotted over to the spot where the Enormous Crocodile was standing, and quick as a flash he wrapped his trunk around the Crocodile's tail and hoisted him up into the air.

"Hey! Let me go!" yelled the Enormous Crocodile, who was now dangling upside down. "Let me go! Let me go!"

"No," Trunky said. "I will not let you go. We've all had quite enough of your clever tricks."

Trunky began to swing the Crocodile round and round in the air. At first he swung him slowly.

Then he swung
him faster…

And FASTER…
And FASTER…

And
FASTER still…

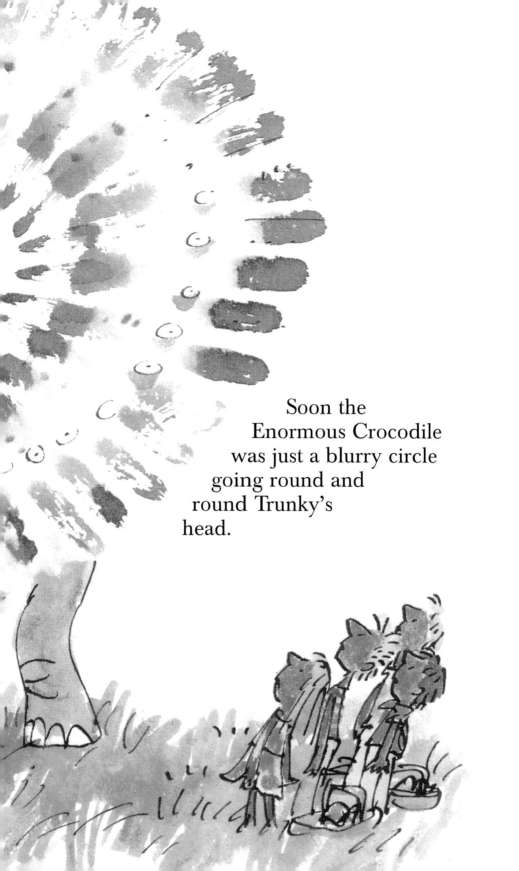

Soon the
Enormous Crocodile
was just a blurry circle
going round and
round Trunky's
head.

Suddenly, Trunky let go
of the Crocodile's tail
and the Crocodile went
shooting high up into
the sky like a huge
green rocket.

Up and up he went...

HIGHER

and

HIGHER...

FASTER

and

FASTER...

He was going so fast
and so high that soon
the earth was just a tiny
dot miles below.

He whizzed on and
on.

He whizzed far into
space.

He whizzed past the
moon.

He whizzed past stars
and planets.

Until at last...

With the most tremendous

BANG!

the Enormous Crocodile crashed
headfirst into the hot hot sun.

And he was sizzled up like a sausage!